A House for Mouse

GABBY DAWNAY

ALEX BARROW

Thames & Hudson

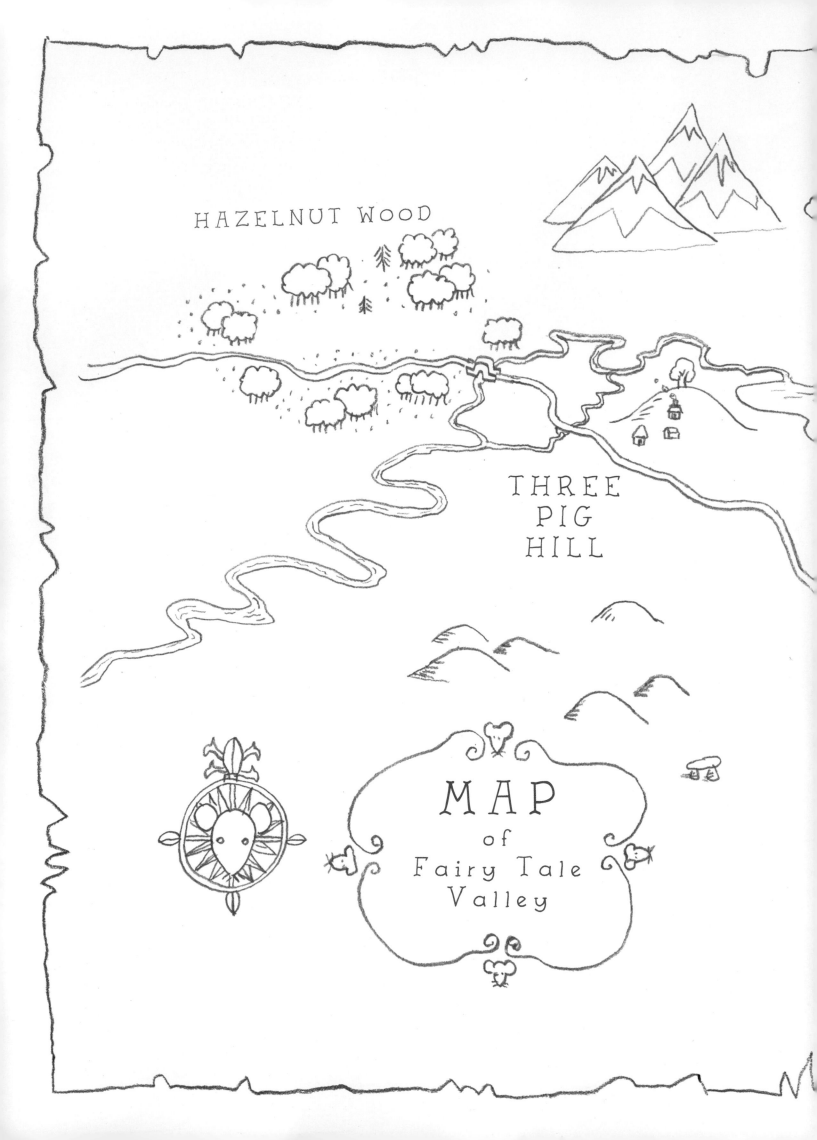

HAZELNUT WOOD

THREE
PIG
HILL

MAP
of
Fairy Tale
Valley

Long, long ago
lived a little gray mouse,
Who decided one day
he must find a new house …

FAREWELL
MOUSE

"I was born in this tree—now it's time to explore
All the nooks and the crannies from forest to shore!"

With a flick of his whiskers and twinkling eyes
He packed up his stuff and he said his goodbyes.

Over mountains and meadows, by road and on track
Went the little gray mouse with his bag on his back.

W̲hen he stopped for a rest and a nibble of nut
He at once saw a house very much like a ... hut!

"It is cosy and warm," thought the mouse, "I can see
That a house made of straw is a great place to be!"

Until all of a sudden there came a loud cough
And before mouse could move, the whole roof had blown off!

"Straw is too dry," thought the mouse, "so are sticks.
Perhaps what I need is a house made of bricks!"

Over mountains and meadows, by road and on track
Went the little gray mouse, with his bag on his back.

While he paused for a moment to chew on a flower,
He looked up at a house that was more like a ... tower.

OLD TOWER

"Just imagine the view,"
    thought the little gray mouse,
"I will find at the top
    of this very tall house!"

Though he searched high and low
and walked all the way round,
The door to this house
was nowhere to be found.

"No way in?" thought the mouse, "That is not very good.
I had better keep house-hunting here in this wood."

As he walked through the trees he could smell something nice ...
Rather sweet, like a cake made of sugar and spice.

"Perhaps it is teatime?" thought little gray mouse
And he followed his nose to a ... gingerbread house!

It was covered in icing and dotted with sweets,
There was chocolate piping and all sorts of treats.

or candy is one giant snack,
...en mouse had a mouthful ... it started to crack.

"Just imagine the mess it would make in the rain!"
Thought the mouse as he started his journey again.

When he next stopped to rest,
sitting down on a root,
He discovered a house
that looked just like a ... boot.

SHOE HOUSE

THE
DARK DARK
WOODS

"A room in a shoe!"
 cried the little gray mouse,
"I feel sure that a shoe
 makes a wonderful house!"

Then he peeped through a window and saw all the toys ...
There were so many children and oh what a no!

"Maybe not," thought the mouse, "It is ever so small.
There is no room for me—there is no room at all!"

"I think pairs are ideal
when it comes to a shoe,
Because one may be fun—
but there's more room in two!"

"No I don't want a cake, or a house made of straw …
And I'd rather not live in a tower with no door."

"Not a single house right—
this is no good at all."
Said the mouse. Then he paused,
as he'd come to a wall.

The wall of a … CASTLE!
Could this be the place?
Oh, the building was perfect—
it had so much space!

What with ballrooms and
turrets, a bedroom—or ten …
"This is IT!" cried the mouse,
"I'm not moving again!"

Then he ran here and there
and all over the house,
"I *know* something's missing,"
said little gray mouse.

For the castle was silent,
as silent as stone
And the little gray mouse
felt so very … alone.

But then all of a sudden
a knock at the door
Sent a BOOM through the castle
from ceiling to floor ...

With a flick of his whiskers
and twinkling eyes
The mouse ran to the door
and then what a ...

"SURPRISE!!!"

... cried his friends,
"We are here and can see
that this castle of yours
is the BEST place to be!"

So they feasted and danced
and they filled it with laughter,
"My house," cried the mouse,
"will be HOME ever after!"

For as far as you move
and wherever you roam,
It is family and friends
who turn house into home.